A Crowded Ride in the Countryside

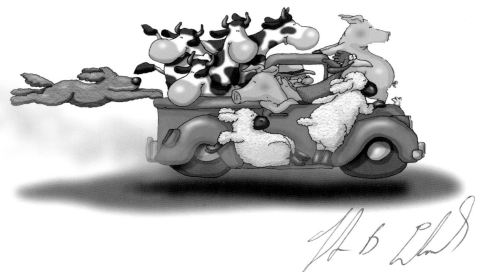

Written by Frank B. Edwards
Illustrated by John Bianchi

Farmer, farmer,
Going to the fair.
Chicken wants a ride . . .

There's room to spare.

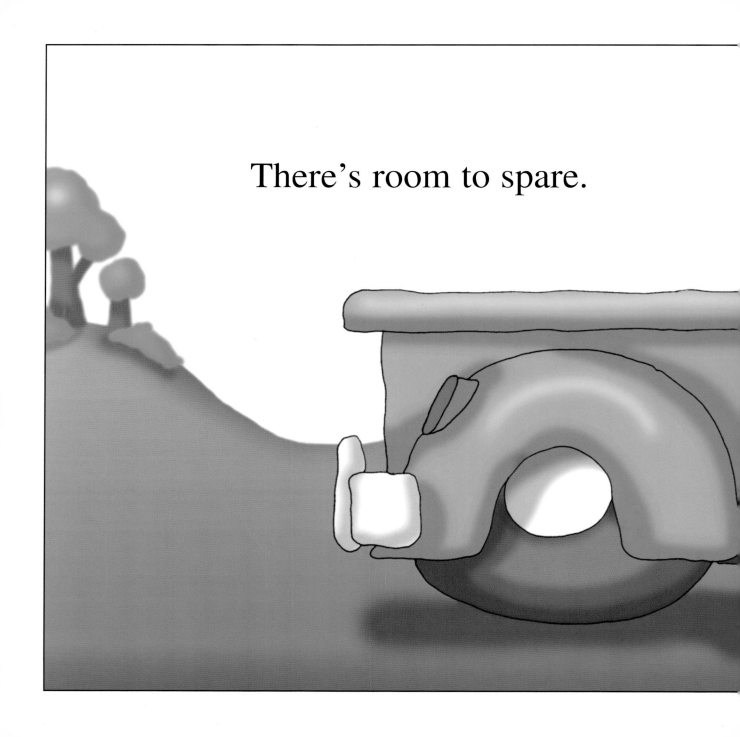

Farmer, farmer,
Going to the fair.
Sheep catch a ride . . .

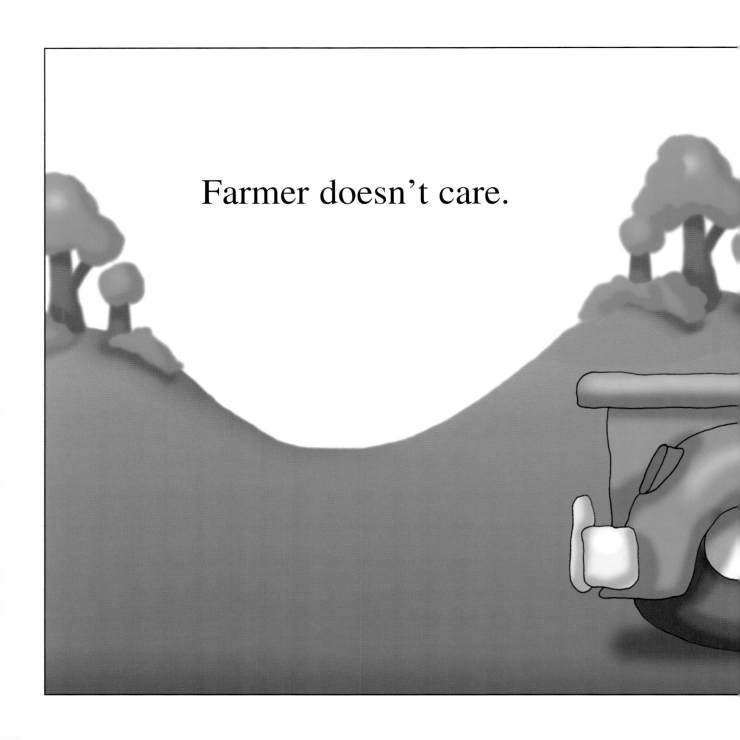
Farmer doesn't care.

Farmer, farmer,
Going to the fair.
Pigs get a ride . . .

Farmer needs some air.

Farmer, farmer,
Going to the fair.
Cows need a ride . . .

Climb on if you dare.

Farmer, farmer,
Going to the fair.
Everyone has to push,
Or he won't get there.

Farmer, farmer,
Going to the fair.
Hits a great big bump,
And flies through the air.

Farmer, farmer,
Landed at the fair.
Everyone has fun,
When they know how to share.

The End